W9-AUE-036

THE HIDDEN BEAST

Don't miss any of the chilling adventures!

SPOOKSVILLE

THE HIDDEN
BEAST

Christopher Pike

Aladdin
NEW YORK LONDON TORONTO SYDNEY NEW DELHI

ALADDIN
An imprint of Simon & Schuster Children's Publishing Division
1230 Avenue of the Americas, New York, NY 10020
This Aladdin hardcover edition April 2016
Text copyright © 1996 by Christopher Pike
Jacket illustration copyright © 2016 by Vivienne To
Also available in an Aladdin paperback edition.
All rights reserved, including the right of reproduction
in whole or in part in any form.
ALADDIN is a trademark of Simon & Schuster, Inc.,
and related logo is a registered trademark of Simon & Schuster, Inc.
For information about special discounts for bulk purchases,
please contact Simon & Schuster Special Sales at 1-866-506-1949
or business@simonandschuster.com.
Jacket designed by Jessica Handelman
Interior designed by Mike Rosamilia
The text of this book was set in Weiss Std.
Manufactured in the United States of America 0316 FFG
2 4 6 8 10 9 7 5 3 1
Library of Congress Control Number 2014946983
ISBN 978-1-4814-1095-3 (hc)
ISBN 978-1-4814-1093-9 (pbk)
ISBN 978-1-4814-1096-0 (eBook)

1

IT WAS LEAH POOLE, BRYCE POOLE'S cousin, who brought the gang the treasure map. The fact that Leah was related to Bryce made Adam Freeman and Watch suspicious. Even though Adam and Watch had shared a couple of adventures with Bryce—one on the other side of the Secret Path, the other when prehistoric dinosaurs invaded Spooksville—the guys simply did not trust Bryce. The fact that he said he wanted to share a treasure with them made them trust him less.

Even the girls had their doubts. While fighting the invasion of dinosaurs, Bryce had made a few bad calls that Sally Wilcox had not forgiven. But to Sally's credit—perhaps a credit to her greed—she was the one most interested in the treasure hunt. Cindy Makey, on the other hand, didn't understand why Leah Poole would go to complete strangers and offer them half of a supposedly fabulous treasure in return for a little help. Cindy liked Bryce, but his cousin was another matter. Yet maybe Cindy's distrust of Leah was partly because Leah was so pretty, with her sandy brown hair and pearl white teeth. Prettier, in fact, than Cindy.

At least that was what Sally later said.

They were in their favorite doughnut shop when Bryce walked in and hit them with the idea of the treasure hunt. Leah was outside for the moment, out of sight. Apparently Bryce wanted to soften them up on the idea first. But he hadn't been talking long when they were all over him with questions.

"Where did this map come from?" Adam asked.

"Where did the treasure come from?" Watch asked.

"Where did Leah come from?" Sally asked.

"Yeah," Cindy echoed.

Bryce shook his head. "One question at a time. First, my cousin was born in Spooksville but moved away five years ago. She's seventeen now, so she left here with my uncle when she was our age. It was her father, Uncle Charlie, who gave her the map just before he died. That was only two months ago—she's still getting over the loss of her dad. It was her dad's dying wish that she return here and find the treasure. Uncle Charlie was flat broke when he died, and Leah has no way to support herself."

"She has no mother?" Cindy asked sympathetically. Blond and cute, Cindy was the gentlest one in the group, except when it came to dealing with Sally.

"Her mother died when she was two," Bryce said. "Anyway, she returned here with this map but . . ."

"Yes?" Adam asked when Bryce didn't finish. Although the shortest and the newest to town, Adam usually led the group.

"It's in code," Bryce said reluctantly.

"And you can't figure it out?" Sally asked. Sally had long brown hair and liked to ask hard questions.

Bryce hesitated. "I am having some difficulties."

"Wonders never cease," Watch said, glancing at one of the four watches he always wore on his arms.

"Where did Leah's father get the map?" Adam asked.

"I don't know," Bryce said. "But he grew up in Spooksville and lived most of his life here. He was adventurous when he was little. I'm not surprised that he found a treasure map."

"But if he's had the map for a while," Watch said, "why didn't he go for the treasure himself?"

"I'm not sure how long he had the map," Bryce said. "I'm only guessing when he got it. He died before Leah could really ask him about it."

Watch frowned. "Are you saying he gave it to her with his dying breath?"

"I wouldn't go that far," Bryce said. "I only know that Leah doesn't know where the map came from."

"Then how does she know it's genuine?" Sally asked.

"Her father swore it was," Bryce said. "I knew the guy. He was honest."

"But we still don't get the deal," Adam said. "Why should Leah share half the treasure with us in exchange for our help? You'll be able to decipher the code without us."

Bryce sighed. "I've been studying the code for the last two weeks and haven't been able crack it yet."

"So it's both a map and directions?" Watch asked.

"Yes," Bryce said. "Leah's outside with the map. She's willing to show it to you, if you swear to keep it secret."

The gang, the inner four, all looked at one another. Sally was the first to speak. "I suppose it couldn't hurt," she said.

"Maybe," Adam answered carefully. "But I've got a funny feeling about this treasure map, even before I see it. Does it hint that there's any danger in chasing after this treasure?"

Again Bryce hesitated. "Sort of. The instructions are weird. There is a hint of danger."

"But why does Leah want us to help?" Watch asked. "We're only kids."

"I told her about you guys," Bryce said. "When it comes to handling bizarre adventures, I said you're the best." He added, "I'm trying to help you, even though you've accused me in the past of acting like I could do everything myself."

"Who accused you?" Adam asked. "Not me."

"Your tone accused me," Bryce said. "Besides, you told me you didn't trust me."

"I think you were the one who said that," Adam said.

"It doesn't matter," Sally said, showing a rare ability to compromise. "We can see the map and then decide if we want to get involved. Who knows—even we may not be able to decode it."

"But if we do decode it," Watch said firmly, "the deal can't change. We get half the treasure."

Bryce nodded. "That's fine with me. If Leah's father was right, there should be so much treasure it won't matter how many share it." Bryce stood. "I'll go get my cousin."

While he was gone, the gang talked.

"Now that I think about it," Watch said, "I do

remember this Leah. She was tall, even as a little kid, and had a sharp mind. I'm surprised she hasn't been able to decode the message."

"Was she a nice person?" Cindy asked.

Watch shrugged. "I didn't really know her."

"Am I a nice person?" Sally asked Cindy with a trace of sarcasm.

Cindy looked her straight in the eye. "One or two days out of the month."

"We only have a few days before school starts," Watch said. "We might want to go on one last summer adventure—all together," he added meaningfully.

Leah appeared a moment later. As Watch remembered, she was tall, with thick red lips and curly hair that seemed to change color as she turned her head in the bright sunlight pouring in through the window. But even though she was five years older, and very pretty, she seemed apprehensive to meet them. She stood stiffly while Bryce introduced her. It was Adam who had to suggest she take a seat. In her hands she carried a brown piece of parchment. As she settled down in the booth across from them, she clutched the paper close to her chest. Watch tried to put her at ease.

"We're not going to steal it from you," he joked. "At least not right away."

Leah smiled thinly. "I haven't told anyone about this map except Bryce. I'm sure you can understand why."

Adam waved his hand. "We're good at keeping secrets. We've had aliens and witches confide in us."

"Not that we confided in them," Sally muttered.

Bryce spoke to Leah. "I'd trust these guys with my life. In fact, they've saved my life. You can trust them with your inheritance."

"Do you think of your treasure map as an inheritance?" Watch asked Leah. "That might not be such a good idea."

"What Watch means is that we might not find anything," Adam said quickly. "We don't want you to be disappointed."

Leah hesitated. "My father said if I could decipher the map, I would find wealth beyond imagination."

"How come he failed to decipher the code?" Sally asked.

"It's not easy," Leah said. "But Bryce tells me you guys are all brilliant."

"Three-quarters of us are," Sally said, glancing at Cindy.

"Let's see the map and we'll show you how brilliant we are," Watch said, obviously anxious to try his wits on the code. Once more Leah hesitated, but then slowly she laid the map down on the table. But it was Adam who spread it open.

The map was simple. On the left side was a series of triangles that seemed to represent mountains. Opposite the triangles was a set of wavy lines that appeared to be the ocean. In between was a bunch of stick trees and what looked like poorly drawn rocks. There was a large X in the middle of the triangles. That was it.

But the clues were bizarre, far from clear.

They were actually written as a poem.

> *When the morning and evening lady stands at*
> *her tallest.*
> *The shadow of the white light of love shall*
> *falleth.*
>
> *In a line of darkness on the door of the smallest.*
> *In a hidden spot on the tallest.*
>
> *Therein lie the jewels that speak in dreams.*
> *The crystals that whisper words that are more*
> *than they seem.*
>
> *But beware the ancient pet.*
> *The fire that burns yet.*

She who remembers old debts.
She whose breath melts every net.

"Nice rhymes," Adam said as he finished reading it out loud. "But I haven't a clue what any of it means."

"Of course you don't," Watch said quickly, taking hold of the map. "We have to study it for a while. But one thing is clear to me. If this is a map of Spooksville, it's reversed. See how the mountains are on the left side, the west side, when they should be on the east side?" Watch frowned. "They're not only reversed. I think they're inverted as well."

"What do you mean?" Cindy asked. "Don't *reversed* and *inverted* mean the same thing?"

"Not exactly," Watch said. "I believe the map was drawn with the help of a mirror. That if we look at its reflection in a mirror we'll see where the X is really supposed to be. Sally, do you know where we can get a mirror?"

"It's not necessary," Bryce said, reaching into his pocket and pulling out a piece of notebook paper. "I've already redrawn the map while looking in a mirror." He opened the folded paper and laid it on the table beside the old parchment. It was an exact copy of the original, but reversed. Bryce smiled. "Very good, Watch. It took me hours studying the map to realize it had been inverted."

Sally wasn't smiling. "Why didn't you volunteer that information from the start?"

Bryce shrugged. "I wanted to see if one of you guys noticed it."

"That's not the way a team works," Adam said in a flat tone. "If you know other things about the map, please tell us now so we don't waste valuable time."

Bryce shook his head. "That's all I know."

Watch continued to study the parchment and the notebook paper intently. He spoke to Bryce with his next question. "But do you know where the X is located?"

Bryce hesitated. "Only approximately."

"Where?" Sally asked.

Watch pointed to the row of triangles. "This is back in the mountains, in a minor range of peaks called the Teeth."

Cindy shuddered. "Why are they called that?"

"Because they're really pointy peaks," Bryce said. "And close together."

"We assume that's the reason," Watch said darkly, staring at Bryce. "This map refers to an ancient pet. Do you have any idea what that means?"

"No," Bryce said. "I haven't been able to figure out the clues."

"Yeah," Sally said sarcastically. "And when you walked in here, you said you didn't know the treasure was located back in the Teeth either."

Bryce held her eye. "I brought Leah and this map to you guys because I trust you. Now gimme a break, will ya?"

"We'll think about it," Sally said.

Adam held up his hand. "Let's look at the clues one by one. What about the first line? 'When the morning and the evening lady stands at her tallest.' That's clearly referring to a special time. Maybe a special time of the day, maybe a special time of the year." He paused. "But which lady is connected to the morning and the evening?"

Cindy shook her head. "I haven't the slightest idea."

"I studied all the different goddesses in mythology," Bryce said. "I couldn't find one that was called the lady of the morning and the evening."

"You studied too hard," Watch said. "The answer is simple."

"It is?" Adam asked. "What is it?"

"The lady referred to here is the planet Venus," Watch said. "The reference in the second line confirms that— 'The shadow of the white light of love shall falleth.' Venus is always associated with love. It is also the only planet in the sky capable of casting shadows on Earth. Few people realize that it can get that bright. But it only casts shadows

11

when it is at its brightest, and when there is no moon. The first line also confirms it must be Venus because the planet is at its brightest when it is farthest from the sun, either as a morning or an evening star."

"When you say it is farthest from the sun, is it highest in the sky?" Adam asked, impressed.

"Yes," Watch said. "In a manner of speaking. Venus is highest—or tallest—when it is far from the sun from our perspective on Earth. Of course, it is always about the same distance from the sun. But from Earth, we see it swing close to and far from the sun."

"How often does this occur?" Adam asked.

Watch shrugged. "A couple times a year, or slightly more often. I'd have to study my books to know for certain. But one thing I do know—Venus is reaching its farthest point from the sun in the morning sky. If you get up early tomorrow, you'll see Venus before the sun rises. It'll be high in the eastern sky, and very bright."

"Is there a moon tonight?" Cindy asked. "Or early tomorrow morning, before it gets light?"

Watch paused. "No."

"Then this is a perfect time to look for the treasure," Sally said, excited.

"Hold on a second," Adam answered. "There are still a lot of clues here that we don't understand. Let's look at the other lines in the first verse. 'In a line of darkness on the door of the smallest. In a hidden spot on the tallest.'" Adam paused. "I assume this means that Venus casts a shadow on some object that points to a door that leads to the treasure."

Watch nodded. "I think it says that and more. It's full of information. I think the smallest is the smallest peak in the Teeth chain of peaks."

"But the hidden spot is on the tallest," Sally said. "That contradicts the previous line."

"Only at first glance," Watch said. "One of the peaks could be the tallest while still being the smallest."

"How?" Cindy asked.

"By being narrow," Watch said. "Even if the peak is tall, it could have the least mass."

"You're so smart, Watch," Cindy said with pleasure.

Sally patted Watch on the back. "Very good. I'm impressed. So now we have the first verse all figured out. But how far back in the mountains are the Teeth?"

Watch frowned. "Way back. We could drive part of the way there, but then we'd have to hike the rest."

"Can we get there in one day?" Adam asked.

"No," Watch said. "If we leave today, we'll have to camp out at least one night and hike the following day."

"But then Venus won't be at its highest point," Sally said. "We won't find what we're looking for."

"Venus won't shift that much in twenty-four hours," Watch explained. "I think these clues give us a window of opportunity of a few days." He paused. "But even if we can identify the correct peak, we might look for days for the right shadow. Unless . . ."

"Unless what?" Adam asked when his friend didn't complete his remark.

"Unless the light or shadow points out another marker," Watch said. "We can hope for that. But let's get back to the other verses. They have me stumped. Jewels that speak in dreams. Crystals that whisper words that are more than they seem. Leah, did your father describe the nature of the treasure?"

"No," she said cautiously. "Not exactly. He just said it was very ancient."

"The last verse speaks of an ancient pet," Sally said.

"And it tells us to beware of her," Adam said. "Maybe we should listen to what it says. She doesn't sound very friendly, not from her description here."

"*She* is probably dead," Sally said. "If the treasure is as old as Leah's father believed."

"Not necessarily," Watch said. "The line 'She who remembers old debts' implies that she lives for a very long time."

Cindy turned to Bryce. "You're really quiet. What do you think about what Watch said?"

Bryce nodded in admiration. "I'm stunned. I think he's figured the whole thing out."

"But I've only figured out the directions on the map," Watch said. "Not the other meanings. Have you any idea what this ancient pet could be?"

"No," Bryce said. "But like Sally, I believe it was something that lived a long time ago. I'm not worried about it."

"I can get a truck," Leah said. "And can drive us." She smiled suddenly. "This is exciting. If we do find the treasure, I think Watch should get an extra big share."

Watch flashed a rare smile. "I wouldn't mind one of those jewels that speaks in dreams."

Leah's smile shrank. "I'm sure we'll find something you like."

Cindy raised an important point. "I don't know about you guys, but I'm going to need time to convince my mom to let me go camping tonight. I won't tell her how far we're going. She'd worry too much."

Adam laughed. "If she only knew how far from home you've been other times, she wouldn't worry about this trip at all." He was referring, of course, to the times they had been in outer space. He added, "My parents will need to be convinced, too."

Sally stood. "My mom and dad like camping, and they'll be happy I'm spending the night with you guys. Don't forget to get your equipment together: sleeping bags, backpacks, and plenty of food and water."

Watch also stood. "I don't have to ask anyone where I can go."

Adam heard the sadness in his friend's voice. He knew that Watch's family was spread all across the country, although he didn't know why. Watch lived with some relative, but Adam forgot who.

"Doesn't anybody ever ask what you do?" Adam asked.

Watch shook his head. "Not usually."

Sally patted Watch on the back and smiled.

"But if you come home with a pile of treasure," she said, "all your relatives will talk to you plenty."

2

IT TOOK THEM LONGER THAN THEY PLANNED to get ready. First, Adam had no equipment, neither a sleeping bag nor a backpack. Sally borrowed stuff from other friends for him. Then Bryce and Leah went off for a long time and didn't return until eleven-thirty. By then Watch was worried they wouldn't even get close to the Teeth before the sun set.

"It really is a hard hike," he said as they climbed in the back of Leah's white truck. Bryce was sitting up front in the cab with his cousin. Watch continued, "The Teeth are pretty high. You have to hike on an incline for a long time. Plus there isn't much water up there. Whenever we come to a stream, we should drink and refill our bottles."

"Are you guys comfortable?" Leah shouted out her window.

"Yeah," Sally said, excited. "We're ready to rock and roll."

Leah started the truck and they headed onto the main road that led out of Spooksville, going north. They were in fact taking the same road Watch had taken when he successfully rescued Cindy from a pterodactyl. But when that road finished this time they'd have to take a dirt road to within twenty miles of the Teeth.

As the warm wind blew in their faces and they veered away from the ocean and their hometown, Adam spoke quietly so that only the four of them could hear.

"Did you notice how little Leah said at our meeting?" he asked.

Watch nodded. "Nothing we said seemed to surprise her much."

"I think she's just shy," Sally said.

Cindy also nodded. "I'm not sure I trust her completely."

"You don't like her because she's prettier than you," Sally said.

Cindy sighed. "Oh brother."

"If I was her," Adam said, "and my own private treasure map had just been decoded, I would have been jumping up and down."

"Maybe she doesn't know how to jump," Sally said.

"Maybe nothing we said was new to her," Watch answered slowly.

"I don't understand," Cindy questioned.

Adam and Watch glanced up front. "I think we should keep an eye on both of them," Adam said.

Sally laughed. "Cindy is already keeping an eye on Bryce. I don't think she ever takes her eyes off him."

Cindy snorted. "Who's the one who gushes over him all the time?"

"Yeah, but he almost got me killed," Sally said. "And he almost destroyed the world in the process. I have trouble forgiving a guy for that."

"Money and treasures bring out the worst in people," Adam said. "We have to watch our backs."

They drove for well over an hour. The bumpy dirt road was more of a path for walking than for driving. Eventually they dead-ended at the sheer side of a rocky cliff. They had gone as far as they could on four wheels and piled out of the truck. Adam helped Cindy on with her pack. She groaned at its weight.

"This thing is heavy," she complained.

"Wait until you're walking up a steep incline with your lips cracked and bleeding and poisonous snakes biting at your exhausted legs," Sally said. "Then it will feel ten times as heavy."

Watch gestured to the sheer cliff in front of them. "We have to hike around this. At first the way is really hard—rocky and steep. Then it levels off some."

Adam tugged on the bill of the cap he had brought to keep the sun off his face. He removed the water bottle from his pack and gulped down a big drink.

"Where's the first place we can stop and refill our bottles?" Adam asked Watch.

"About four hours from here," Watch said, once more checking his watches. "We won't get there until around five. But we can't stop there, not if we plan to get to the Teeth by tomorrow morning, early enough to catch Venus in the dark sky."

"I'm confused," Cindy said. "I thought we weren't going to try to search until the morning after?"

"We'll see how far we get today," Leah interrupted.

"Yeah," Bryce agreed. "Let's play it by ear."

They started off. As Watch had said the way was grueling at first. Several times Cindy slipped on loose gravel and scratched her knees. Because it was hot, she was wearing shorts and the scratches were rather nasty. They had to stop while she bandaged them. Luckily Sally had remembered to bring a first-aid kit.

Sally was the most comfortable hiking. In fact, she was the most experienced climber, even though she didn't know these mountains as well as Watch. For the most part it was Sally and Watch who led. Sally talked about what she'd buy if they did find the treasure, as they moved steadily upward.

"The first thing I want is a house in a town other than Spooksville," she said. "Then I'd be able to sleep peacefully at night and not have to worry about whether I'd be dead in the morning."

"But if you moved to another town," Adam said, trudging along behind her, "we'd miss you. And you would miss all our great adventures."

Sally laughed. The mountain air seemed to put her in a good mood.

"I could come back and visit whenever you needed me," she said.

"But we need you every day," Cindy gasped, bringing up the rear.

"We're forgetting that some of this treasure might be of historical significance," Watch said. "In that case we might be obligated to donate at least a portion of it to a museum."

"We're not donating any of my treasure to a museum," Leah interrupted.

Watch was not taken aback. "I was speaking of our half. I assume we can do whatever we want with it."

Leah glanced at him and her pretty green eyes flashed with light. But whether it was a harsh light or a gentle one Adam wasn't sure. Leah gave a quick smile and spoke in a gentler voice.

"Of course you can do whatever you want with your share," she said.

The area had been largely dry and barren, but now they were beginning to pass some trees. The high green branches, although sparse, provided welcome shade. The ground began to level out and even Cindy got a second wind. They began to walk faster, and talk less, and for three continuous hours made excellent time. Indeed, they came to the waterhole Watch had described twenty minutes ahead of schedule. It was a shallow but clear pool that was formed by a spring that seemed to shoot straight out from the side of a cliff. As they kneeled to refill their bottles, Adam was pleased to see their reflections in the pool.

"Look!" he exclaimed. "Before anyone touches the water. There we are—there are two of each of us now."

Sally crouched beside him and made a face at her reflection. "I wish I'd brought my camera," she said. "It's beautiful here."

"It is very peaceful," Cindy agreed, picking a flower and smelling it.

Bryce threw his pack down beside the pool. "We mustn't take any pictures of the treasure," he said. "We mustn't ever let anyone know what we have found."

"We understand," Watch said.

Bryce glanced at him. "Just wanted to make sure we're on the same wavelength."

They rested for half an hour before starting out again. Now, according to Watch, they were entering an area even he didn't know well. Yet he apparently did have an idea of where he wanted to camp for the night.

"There is a large bowl-like valley at the foot of the Teeth," he said. "We'll be sheltered from the wind and hopefully from any wild animals."

"Are there wild animals up here?" Cindy asked nervously.

"Just mountain lions and brown bears," Sally said. "Adam, did you bring your laser pistol?"

"No," Adam said.

Leah frowned. "Do you really have a laser pistol?"

"Yeah, he does," Sally said with a laugh. "He stole it from an alien seventy million years ago."

Bryce turned to Leah. "I told you they had been interesting places," he said.

They reached the bowl-like valley at eight o'clock. Now they had less than half an hour of light left to set up camp. It would be hardly enough. But the group worked well together, and soon they had their tents and sleeping bags nicely laid out. They even started a fire and heated up a dinner of soup and beans in the crackling flames. Cindy had brought along bags of chips to share.

Above them the black silhouette of the Teeth waited for them. There were six peaks altogether, but the farthest one was clearly the tallest and the narrowest. Cindy pointed to it as they ate.

"How far away would you say that is, Watch?" she asked.

"At least six miles," he said. "Maybe more. I don't think we should try for it in the morning before dawn. It would be better to hike to it after the sun comes up and try to find the treasure the following morning."

"Do you think that's wise?" Bryce asked. "The clues were specific. We should be there when Venus is at its highest, which you say is tomorrow morning."

"But, as I explained, I don't think it'll make much difference," Watch said. "Besides, to hike there in the early morning hours, in the pitch-black before the sun rises, could be dangerous. One slip and someone could break a leg or be killed."

"Wouldn't the police send a helicopter back to rescue us?" Cindy asked.

"Not the Spooksville police," Sally said. "They're all afraid of heights."

"And the dark," Watch added.

Bryce glanced at Leah. "I don't agree with this," he said. "What do you think?"

Leah shrugged and stared at the farthest peak, which was so narrow and tall it looked unnatural. "If Watch says it's too dangerous, I agree with him." She raised a hand to stifle a yawn. "Besides, I'm exhausted. I'm not used to this much exercise. I want to sleep for ten hours straight. I don't want to get up in the middle of the night to hike in the dark to an unfamiliar place."

"All right," Bryce said reluctantly. "If that's the feeling of the whole group."

"I agree with Watch," Sally said quickly.

"So do I," Adam said. "Safety first."

"A difficult motto to live by in Spooksville," Cindy said. Then she added, "Do we need to have someone stand guard? Against wild animals, I mean?"

Watch shook his head. "If we keep the fire going, it

will keep any animals away. To be sure it doesn't go out, I'll set an alarm on one of my watches so I can get up and put a few logs on it."

"What time will you be getting up?" Leah asked.

Watch shrugged. "Maybe two in the morning. Why?"

"I was just wondering," Leah replied.

3

ADAM WAS DREAMING ABOUT FIRE WHEN HE was roughly shaken. He was almost relieved to be awake. The dream had not been pleasant, more of a nightmare really. It was as if everything he loved and cherished in life had been burned to a crisp by some incredible force.

He sat up and found Watch staring at him in the dark. The fire had burned down low; it was little more than glowing cinders. The dim red light heightened the worried expression on his friend's face.

"What's the matter?" Adam asked anxiously.

"Leah's gone," Watch said.

"Are you sure? Maybe she just had to go to the bathroom."

"No. She's been gone too long."

Adam wiped at his eyes and glanced up at the Teeth. It was still pitch-black. There were a million stars in the sky, like bright dots on a black painting. The stars traced an unearthly outline of the peaks.

"How long is long?" Adam asked.

"I've been up fifteen minutes," Watch said. "She's been gone at least that long."

"Why didn't you wake me sooner?"

"Because I kept thinking she'd come back." Watch paused and sighed. "I should have known."

"What?"

"That she would double-cross us. I suspected that she'd already figured out the map long before she met with us yesterday morning."

"Then why bring us along?" Adam asked.

"There could be a lot of reasons. She obviously doesn't know this area as well as I do. She may have used us to get this far. Also, she might want to use us for something yet to come."

"So you definitely think she's set out for the tall peak?"

"I haven't the slightest doubt of it. Do you?"

Adam hesitated. "No. Is Bryce here? Are they in this together?"

28

Watch gestured. "He's sleeping sound as a baby. But that doesn't mean anything."

Adam understood. "He could have stayed behind to fake us out."

"Exactly."

"What should we do?" Adam asked.

Watch drew in a deep breath and frowned. He studied the nearby peaks.

"I still think it's dangerous to try to scale any of these peaks in the dark," he said. "But if we want to get our share of the treasure, we might not have a choice."

"Do we care about the treasure?" Adam asked. "Is it worth risking our lives?"

"It's more the principle of the thing," Watch said. "Leah made a deal with us. She should keep her end of the bargain. I hate to see her get away with her scheme."

"The two of us could go after her alone," Adam suggested. "We could leave the others a note."

Watch shook his head. "The girls would be mad. They'd accuse us of being sexist. Or at least Sally would. Plus there *is* safety in numbers. I say we either all go or all stay. I don't think we should separate."

Adam pointed to a bright white star low in the eastern sky.

"Is that Venus?" he asked.

"Yes. See how bright it is."

"How long till the sun comes up?"

"Three hours. But we really only have two if we're to catch any shadows Venus casts on the tall peak. Once the dawn begins to break, the shadows will vanish." He paused. "Leah must have known that."

Adam nodded. "She must have known a lot more than we thought."

"Yeah. She may even know what the ancient pet really was. Maybe her father told her." Watch added, "Maybe that's the other reason we're here."

Adam didn't like the sound of that.

Hiking toward the tall peak in the pitch-black turned out to be as difficult as Watch feared. Even though they had a couple of flashlights, they kept bumping into one another and sliding on loose gravel. When they started up the actual peak, the way became even more treacherous. The mountain had no path to the top. They found themselves clinging to rocky ledges they could hardly see. And the worst thing was they weren't even sure where they were going.

"How do we know this supposed doorway isn't lower down on the peak?" Sally asked Watch, who carried one of the flashlights in his free hand.

"We don't," Watch said. "But it seems logical the important spot should be high up."

"Why?" Cindy gasped, laboring beside Adam, who carried the other light. They had brought three flashlights, but Leah took one.

"Because between us and Venus is another peak," Watch explained. "It's only when we get near the top that the planet's light will shine clearly on this peak."

"It's hard to believe Leah went all this way by herself," Bryce said.

"Believe it, buster," Sally snapped. "She stabbed us in the back. Are you sure you didn't know what she was up to?"

"I've already answered that question three times," Bryce muttered.

"But how couldn't you know?" Sally insisted. "She's your cousin. You were always off talking to her alone."

"I don't know Leah that well," Bryce said. "She only just returned to town."

"I bet no matter what happens, you end up with your share of the treasure," Sally said.

"Cut it out," Adam said. "We're together now. We have to work together. If Leah did try to go this way by herself, she could be in danger."

"Like I'm dying to rescue her," Sally said.

Because the peak was so narrow it looked taller than it was. An hour of hard climbing brought them close to the top. They stopped short of the summit because they suddenly came to a ledge of rock that was smooth and flat, at least twenty feet square. As they pulled themselves up on the smooth ground, they were sure they had arrived at the right place.

In the center of the flat square was a single smoothly polished boulder. On top of it, standing on edge, was a smaller circular stone with a hole in the center of it. Behind these stones was another rock. Unlike the two center stones, it seemed to have been recently placed there. Watch studied the collection of rocks, straightened his thick lenses, and pointed at Venus, which shone in the eastern sky like a warning beacon.

"The light of Venus, if I am correct, should pass directly through the hole in this small stone," he said. "That should create a round shadow—defined by the white light—that should trace a circle on the cliff here."

"You mean this will happen if you take away the rock behind the other two?" Adam asked.

"Yes," Watch replied.

"You think Leah placed that rock there to block the shadow from forming?" Sally asked.

"I'm sure of it," Watch said. "The other two rocks look

as if they were carved there, thousands of years ago. But the small stone seems to mess up the arrangement."

"Take it away," Cindy said. "Let's see what happens."

Watch reached out and removed the rock. The white light of Venus pierced the hole in the center of the circle. Its rays, as they flared out on either side, described a perfect circle of shadow and light, a circle as tall as a man.

Then they heard a noise.

It scared them so badly they almost backed off the edge of the cliff.

The wall of the cliff began to creak and groan.

And a door began to open.

It was circular, the exact same circle as drawn by the light of Venus. It swung open like a regular door. When it was through moving, they cautiously moved to the opening and peered into a blackness so deep it made the surrounding night seem bright. Inside, a path definitely led down; the steps that sloped away from them into the center of the peak fell off at a steep angle. The beams of their two flashlights played over the stone steps for a short distance before being lost in the blackness.

"I think they go down a long way," Adam said in a quiet voice.

"It looks like it," Watch agreed.

"I wonder if Leah has been here already," Bryce questioned.

"She could have been here and already be gone," Watch said. "How do we know she didn't hike here the minute we were all asleep?"

Bryce shook his head. "I don't think so. If she is here, I think we'll find her inside."

"Are we going inside?" Cindy asked, concerned.

"We didn't hike all the way here to admire the exterior door," Sally said. Then she glanced at Watch and Adam. "But if you guys want me to stand guard outside here, I don't mind."

"Coward," Cindy whispered.

"Who are you calling a coward?" Sally snapped.

"The two of us," Cindy said. "I'd prefer to stay and stand guard with you." She paused. "Who knows? The door might suddenly shut behind us."

Watch nodded. "Cindy has a point. It might be foolish for us all to go inside."

"And it might be dangerous for us to separate," Adam countered. "I prefer we stay together."

"Are you saying that because you don't trust me?" Bryce asked.

"I never said anything about trust," Adam replied, although the thought had crossed his mind.

"If we're going in, let's get going," Watch said. "I want to see where these steps lead."

Sally was excited. "Obviously they lead to the treasure."

"Yeah," Adam muttered. "But to what else?"

THE DESCENT WAS LONG AND DIFFICULT.
Because the angle was so steep, they were constantly
afraid of slipping and falling. Also, the deeper they
went, the damper the steps became. Soon the smooth
surface of each step was covered with a thin layer of
liquid that squished under the soles of their shoes.

Eventually, however, the steps leveled off and
they came to a cavern with a large dark pool at its
center. The walls of the cavern disappeared into the
darkness. The pool lay to either side of them, dark
liquid that showed no bottom when they shone their
flashlights into it. Indeed, they couldn't even see the
edges of it with their lights. Sally leaned over and

touched the liquid and put a handful up to her nose.

"It's just water," she said. "But it's got a faint odor that I can't place."

Cindy took a step back. "I don't think you should disturb it."

"A pool of water can't hurt us," Sally said, although she did step back.

"Unless an ancient pet sleeps beneath it," Watch said ominously.

Adam glanced at him. "You don't think it's here?"

Watch glanced around. "If it does exist, it's in here somewhere. The less we disturb the better."

"I'm worried about Leah," Bryce said with genuine concern. "I'd like to call out for her."

"Don't you dare," Watch said strictly, his meaning clear. If the ancient pet was here, and asleep, there was no need to wake it up.

They went on, and soon it became clear that the cavern they had entered was vast. But the darkness was oppressive. Their voices, as they whispered, died in the air above and around them. It was as if a huge invisible presence hung over them. Yet they could see and hear nothing. The dampness on the ground remained.

For a moment, behind them in the distance, they thought they saw a flicker of light. It caused them all to stop.

"That could be a flashlight," Adam gasped.

"Leah," Watch agreed.

The light winked out as quickly as it had gone on.

"She may have circled around us," Sally said. "She may already be on her way out with the treasure."

"She might shut the door on us," Cindy said.

"Leah won't hurt us," Bryce said.

"Leah has already lied to us," Sally said.

"If she is on her way out," Adam said, "let's be happy she's safe and let her go."

"I agree," Watch said. "We've come this far, so we might as well see what's in this cavern."

They hadn't walked much farther when they became aware of something huge waiting in the darkness in front of them. The realization came slowly because at first their minds refused to accept what they were hearing. It sounded like the long, slow breathing of a creature as large a dozen houses.

They stopped in their tracks.

The deep breathing sounded like horror.

Whistling in and out of lungs that had to be as big as factory furnaces.

"What is that?" Sally whispered anxiously.

"It's something large," Adam whispered. "That's for sure."

"Probably large and ancient," Watch said.

"The ancient pet?" Cindy gasped.

"It has to be," Watch said.

"We have to go back," Cindy said quickly.

"We don't need any treasure this much," Sally agreed.

"What do you think?" Watch asked Adam.

But before Adam could reply Bryce spoke.

"Whatever it is, it sounds as if it's asleep," he said. "We should be able to go around it."

"But if we wake it," Adam said, "it could kill us."

"I'm willing to take that risk," Bryce said.

"You don't even know what you're risking," Adam snapped. "You don't know what it is."

"We could shine our lights on it," Cindy said.

Simultaneously the rest of them said, "No!"

Sally added, "Do any of you notice how hot it has gotten since we first heard it?"

"'But beware the ancient pet,'" Watch quoted. "'The fire that burns yet.'" He added, "Do you guys see a faint red glow coming from the direction of it?"

Adam squinted. "There is something there. A fire perhaps."

Cindy fretted. "We can't just stand here talking. Let's either go around it or go back. I'm for going back."

"I will not go back," Bryce said flatly.

"You realize that you are forcing us to go with you," Watch said.

"How?" Bryce demanded.

"We can't leave you alone," Watch said.

"I don't mind," Cindy said.

"Look," Adam said. "Let's sneak up and see how much room we have to move around it. For all we know this creature takes up all of the cavern in front of us. Even you, Bryce, wouldn't try to walk *over* it."

They headed to the left of the thing in front of them. To their relief the cavern was wide enough to let them pass, and soon the creature was slumbering behind them, still off to their right. But the sound of it receding behind them was not all that comforting.

"We'll have to go past it again," Cindy said.

"Perhaps," Watch said. "It's this creature that guards the treasure. Remember the next to the last line. 'She who remembers old debts.'"

"If that's true," Adam said, "and if we find the treasure, we might not want to touch it."

"We're never going to find anything in all this darkness," Sally said.

"Except maybe our deaths," Cindy added quietly.

Sally was wrong. Not long after passing the sleeping beast, the cavern narrowed and they entered a space that was no bigger than a school gymnasium. As they panned their flashlights around, they jumped, listening to their own hearts pound in wonder and amazement.

The room was filled with treasure.

Gold coins and bars, piled in hills that reached to the black ceiling, surrounded them. And jewels in every color of the rainbow glistened in the sea of yellow. There were even pearls, strung on exquisite chains and wrapped around tiny but precious statues of jade. Truly, they had found the riches of the ages.

Yet all the wealth seemed to be gathered as a mere ornament to glorify a couple of foot-tall crystals that stood in the center of the room on a pedestal made of silver. They were narrow, rising up to sharp tips. As they drew near, they saw that special grooves had been carved in the silver stand to support the crystals.

Yet there were four grooves and only two crystals.

Watch spoke softly in the darkness.

"'Therein lie the jewels that speak in dreams,'" he said. "'The crystals that whisper words that are more than they seem.'"

"And two of them are missing," Sally added.

"Leah wouldn't have taken them," Bryce said quickly.

"No?" Adam said. "Two of them have obviously been removed. And you did say you hardly knew her."

"The code seemed to indicate that the crystals were the most valuable things here," Watch said.

"Then why didn't she take all of them?" Bryce asked.

"It would be hard enough for her to hike with even two of them on her," Watch said. "I think she took as many as she could carry."

Cindy gestured to the other treasure. "But there are so many gems here, so much gold—why fool with the crystals? I mean, we don't even know what they can do."

"But I'm betting Leah does," Adam said. "Her father told her more than we know." He paused, "Is that possible, Bryce?"

Bryce was at a loss. "She didn't tell me anything."

"Then why do you keep defending her?" Sally asked.

"She's my cousin!" Bryce snapped. "Family. Wouldn't you defend your family?"

"I would," Watch said softly, even though his family was spread all over the country.

"We're not trying to pick on you," Adam told Bryce. "We're just trying to figure out what to do next."

"I say we take these two crystals," Sally said. "And stuff our pockets with as many diamonds and emeralds and rubies as we can carry."

"But what about the monster out there?" Cindy asked.

Sally made a face. "He's probably been in here for

thousands of years. What's he going to spend all this wealth on?"

"No," Adam said. "We know nothing about this creature, except that the treasure probably belongs to him."

"I think it's a her," Watch corrected.

"It doesn't matter," Adam continued. "If we take any of this stuff, it will be stealing."

"You cannot steal from a beast," Sally complained. "They have no constitutional rights."

"Couldn't we just take a few emeralds?" Cindy asked Adam, apparently having a sudden change of heart. "I've always loved emeralds, and there are so many of them."

"I can't tell any of you what to do," Adam said. "But I feel it's wrong. If there hadn't been a sleeping beast, I might have felt different. But now I feel like we are breaking and entering."

"I wouldn't go that far," Watch said, stepping closer to the crystals. He peered at them for a moment before frowning. "This is odd."

"What?" Bryce asked.

"These appear to be nothing more than quartz," Watch said. "The least valuable thing in this room. Yet they're placed here on a pedestal, and the code implied they are magical."

"We haven't had good luck in the past with magical devices," Cindy warned.

"We could take just one," Sally said as she reached forward to pick one up.

"Don't!" Watch snapped, trying to stop her.

He was too late.

Sally already held the crystal in her hands.

She laughed at their concern. "It's not like this is a weapon."

But it must have been something important.

Behind them they heard the sleeping beast begin to stir.

5

A RHYTHMIC CHANGE IN THE BREATHING OF the beast was the only difference. It was no longer slow and deep but rough and—it actually sounded—grumpy. From this they assumed it was waking up, but of course they still couldn't see it to be sure. Sally put down the crystal and wiped her hands on her pants.

"I was just looking at it," she said quickly.

Watch hastened to the entryway of the treasure room and peered into the blackness. Adam came up at his side.

"What's happening?" Adam whispered.

"I don't know," Watch replied. "But I think it's more than a coincidence that the beast stirred the moment

Sally touched the crystal. I agree with you now, Adam. I think we'd be crazy to try to take any of this treasure."

"Maybe it wouldn't mind if we just took a handful of diamonds," Sally said behind them.

Adam walked back to the others. He pointed a finger at Sally. "Don't even think about it. In fact, Cindy, Bryce—keep an eye on Sally's hungry hands."

Sally was insulted. "I wouldn't do anything behind your backs."

Watch rejoined them. "We're just trying to be sure." He paused. In the distance, it sounded as if the beast were once again falling asleep. Watch continued, "Now might be the time to get out of here."

Cindy kept looking at the gems. "It's so sad to leave all this behind."

Sally put her hands on her hips. "Who should be watching who? I saw Cindy slip an emerald in her pocket."

"That's a lie!" Cindy snapped. Then she paused and opened her right fist. "I was just looking at the stone. I wasn't going to take it. I never put it in my pocket."

"Then put it back where you found it and let's get out of here," Adam said.

Bryce paused beside the crystals. "I would really like to know what these are capable of doing."

Sally took his arm and led him toward the entrance

with the rest of the gang. "Maybe in another lifetime you can find out," she said.

They reentered the huge cavern, and at first everything seemed okay. The huge invisible beast was clearly asleep once more, so they hurried back the way they had come, first finding the dark pool. Perhaps, in the black, they would have gotten lost had it not been for the vigilance of Watch, who had kept track of their route on a compass on one of his watches.

"I'm glad someone was thinking," Adam said, complimenting his friend for his quick thinking. "I would hate to be trapped in here forever."

"We still have to see if the door is open," Sally said.

"Leah wouldn't shut it on us," Bryce said again.

"But does she know we're in here?" Adam worried aloud. "She could shut it without knowing about us."

"Or maybe the door just shuts by itself when the sun comes up," Watch warned.

They started up the long steps. Going up was definitely harder than going down. Soon they were huffing and puffing. Adam was sweating so badly that he finished his water bottle before they were even halfway up. The slippery stone steps continued to be a problem. They had to use extra effort to keep from sliding backward and tumbling down.

Yet after half an hour of climbing they caught sight of a glow up ahead. They knew it was the door open to the daytime sky. Watch had to tell them what they had only suspected.

"We've been underground for three hours," he said.

"That's incredible," Cindy answered. "It didn't feel half that long."

"Traveling underground can have that effect on the mind," Watch said. "Miners say that all the time. Time gets distorted in the brain. The opposite effect can also happen. Underground, an hour can seem like a whole day."

The light drew them forward, and they climbed with renewed vigor. Indeed, they congratulated themselves that they had found the treasure, faced the ancient beast, and escaped without any permanent harm. They had finally had an adventure that was harmless.

But then the door up ahead began to close.

At this point Watch and Cindy were trailing behind the others. The scratches Cindy had received the previous day had begun to bother her. As a result she was moving slowly, and Watch had dropped back to make sure she was okay. When the door above them began to shut, Watch and Cindy were at least one minute behind the others. Adam realized in an instant that Sally and

Bryce and he might be able to make it out, but his other friends were in danger of getting trapped. He whirled around and shouted down to them.

"It's closing! Hurry!"

Watch and Cindy found renewed vigor.

They began to run up the steps—two and three at a time.

"Don't wait for us!" Watch yelled. "Get out!"

Adam was indecisive, but Sally and Bryce were running toward the door as if their lives depended on reaching it.

"I don't want to leave you!" Adam called down.

"Get to the door!" Watch yelled up. "Hold it open for us!"

Adam realized his friend was right. He couldn't help them by waiting on the steps for them to catch up. He had to get to the door and brace it somehow to keep it from closing. He called down one last time before turning and racing after Sally and Bryce.

"Don't stop for anything!" Adam said.

As Adam pounded toward the door, he saw that it was moving slowly, as if responding to some internal trigger. It was only because the door was taking time closing that any of them had a chance of getting out.

Adam saw Sally and Bryce disappear through the

opening to the outside. Then he saw them gripping the edge of the door in an effort to prevent it from closing. But it was stronger than their flesh and blood muscles.

"We can't hold it!" Sally screamed. "Adam!"

"Brace it with a stone!" Adam yelled.

"We can't let go!" Bryce called back. "It will just close!"

"It's closing anyway!" Adam gasped, twenty steps from the top. "Get a rock!"

But either Sally and Bryce were too afraid to let go or else Bryce was right that it would have closed the moment they released it. In either case they continued to struggle with it, and at the last possible second Adam was able to squeeze through to the outside. He barely made it. The tail of his shirt, in fact, got caught in the hard edge of the door and he had to remove the shirt just to be free of the cliff wall.

Of course that was the least of his worries.

His friends were trapped inside.

And none of them had any idea how to open the door now that Venus was no longer visible in the bright sky. Indeed, they had to wonder if it would be another six months before the door could be opened.

6

ADAM PACED RESTLESSLY ALONG THE STONE ledge. Bryce and Sally sat quietly. Ten minutes had gone by since the door had closed. During that time they had tried as hard as they could to reopen the door. The only problem was that it seemed to have disappeared. On the sheer cliff wall, there wasn't even an outline of it. Not only could they not get a grip on it, they couldn't even say exactly where it had been.

"You should have braced it open with a rock," Adam muttered.

"There wasn't time," Bryce said.

"Because you wasted your time trying to hold it open," Adam shot back.

"Stop it," Sally said in a soft voice. "We both did what we could, Adam, and you know that. If we had not pulled back on it as we did, and slowed it down, you wouldn't have got out."

Adam stopped pacing and nodded weakly.

"You're right. I'm sorry," he said. "I shouldn't have snapped at you."

Bryce stood and sighed. "It's all right. I can't blame you. I got you guys into this mess."

Sally also stood. "No, you didn't. It's Leah who's to blame."

Adam surveyed the hills and valleys far below. With the sun up, the view was stunning. But obviously Adam couldn't enjoy it. Watch and Cindy were trapped in the dark with some beast. That's all Adam could think about. They might be only a few feet away, waiting for Adam to reopen the door. But Adam could hear no one, and he certainly couldn't help them.

There was no sign of Leah.

"I wonder where she is," Adam said.

"She's probably on her way back to the truck," Bryce said.

"Then you finally admit she stabbed us in the back?" Sally said.

Bryce nodded reluctantly. "I guess so."

"If she takes the truck," Adam said, "it'll take us for-ever to get back."

Sally was shocked. "You want to go back? You just want to leave Watch and Cindy trapped inside?"

Adam felt too weary to argue. "Do we have a choice?"

"Yes," Sally said. "We stay and search for another way in."

Bryce shook his head. "Adam is right. Searching for another way in will be just a waste of time. That cavern was far underground, and the tunnel itself had no other tunnels leading into it."

Sally stared at them, amazed. "I can't believe you guys are just going to give up on them."

Adam spoke impatiently. "We're not giving up on them. Back in town we can find something that can blast through this stone wall. We might even be able to use a jackhammer on it. But staying here makes no sense."

"The door could open again," Sally said. "We don't know everything that might trigger its lock."

"We can sit around and wait for magic to happen that might not even exist," Adam said.

Bryce walked to the edge of the cliff and looked

down. "If we're even to stand a chance of getting back to town today, we should leave now."

Adam patted Sally on the shoulder. "We'll get them out of there. Don't worry."

Sally glanced nervously at the spot where the door had been.

"I just hope that beast doesn't wake up hungry," she said.

Inside in the dark Watch and Cindy rested on the steps and tried to figure out what they should do and what their friends would do. Cindy was reluctant to leave the vicinity of the door, but Watch felt they had no choice but to leave.

"But they might be forcing the door open right now," Cindy said. "Why shouldn't we wait for them?"

"You forget what the door looked like before we opened it," Watch said.

"What did it look like?" Cindy asked.

"Nothing. There was just rock wall."

"But we were looking at it in the dark."

"It doesn't matter. I studied it as soon as we climbed up on the ledge. I suspect that once the door closes, it vanishes. Even if they're able to find a stick, I doubt that they'd be able to lever it open. I think that they'll hike back to town. They may even try to reach the truck before Leah does. It's possible they could, if they hurry." He paused. "That's what I'd try to do, and Adam is no fool."

"But they should be able to find something in town that can open the door, don't you think?" Cindy asked hopefully.

Watch wanted to be encouraging, although he thought they were probably doomed already. The stone door had been three feet thick. He smiled and patted her arm.

"Sure," he said. "They know where we are. They'll get to us eventually."

"Then why do you want to leave this place? If they return, we won't know it."

Watch held up his flashlight and water bottle. The former had begun to dim slightly and the latter was completely empty.

"If we're going to explore to try to find another way out," Watch said, "we should do it now, while we have some strength left and our light is still working. Also, we need to go back down and fill up our water bottles."

"From the dark pool?" she asked anxiously.

"Yes."

"I didn't like the look of that water."

"We have no choice," Watch said. "The climb up these steps has left me dehydrated. I'm sure you're no better off. We'll need our strength to search for another exit. We have to drink the water and hope it's okay."

"Could there be another way out? Or in? Won't the others stay and search for another entrance?"

"Of course there could be another entrance, but it will be easier for us to find it than for the others to search the whole mountain looking for it. They should come to that same conclusion. That's why I'm sure they'll head back."

Cindy groaned as she glanced at the stone wall. There was no sign that there had ever been a door there.

"This reminds me of the time we were trapped in the Haunted Cave," she said.

"And you escaped from there."

Cindy smiled. "Yeah. After almost getting killed a few times." She paused. "Do you think that beast has been asleep for thousands of years?"

"It's hard to imagine that any creature could sleep that long. It's possible that it wakes up from time to time and stretches and goes for a swim."

"And checks on its treasure?" Cindy asked.

Watch nodded gravely. "I wish Leah hadn't taken

the two crystals. I wish Sally hadn't even touched the remaining two." He stood and offered her his hand. "Come on, we can talk ourselves to death. We'll feel better when we're doing something."

They started back down the steps. But they moved slowly. They were thirsty and tired, and despite Watch's encouraging words, a blanket of gloom hung over them. At least the tunnel was wide enough so that they could walk together and give each other physical as well as mental support. Although neither of them said it out loud, both continued to strain with their ears, hoping that the door would suddenly open somehow and free them.

After a time they reached the dark pool and kneeled beside it with their empty water bottles. In the light of their only flashlight, there was no mistaking Cindy's reluctance.

"It could be poisoned," she said.

"There's no reason to think it is. If the beast who lives here drinks from this pool, it would need fresh water." He touched it with his hand and raised his damp fingers to his lips. He licked them. "It seems all right."

"Sally said it had a slight smell?"

Watch sniffed at his hands. "It does but it's a nice smell. To tell you the truth, this water tastes better than the stuff we have in town." He paused. "But if it would make you feel better, I'll drink first and you can wait for a few minutes and see if my face melts off or an alien monster jumps out of my guts."

Cindy laughed softly. "I am actually more worried that the water will turn you into an alien monster."

Watch smiled. "I suffered that fate long ago, didn't you know? That's why my family all moved away. They were afraid I wasn't human."

Cindy heard the pain in his voice even while he was trying to make a joke. She reached out and touched his hand.

"Why did they all move away?" she asked gently.

He just smiled again, but looked away.

"Well, you know Spooksville," he said. "It's a dangerous place."

"Watch, tell me, if you can."

He lowered his head. "I can't tell you now, Cindy. But maybe another time. Would that be all right?"

She leaned over and hugged him. "Sure. I just worry about you is all."

He looked up. "Really?"

"Yeah. Why do you sound surprised?"

He shrugged, although it was clear he was embarrassed.

"I don't know," he said. "I've just never had anyone who worried about me before."

"That's because you never had friends like us before," Cindy said seriously. "And I'm sorry if I was prying. I only ask because I worry that you're sad sometimes, you know, and you might feel that you have no one to talk to about it. What I mean is, you can talk to me whenever you want. About anything."

Watch hugged her back and spoke in her ear.

"I'll tell you a secret," he said. "I'm never sad around you guys."

"Good," Cindy said, and she meant it.

They each drank from the dark pool and refilled their water bottles. Soon they felt refreshed. Watch was right, Cindy thought. The water was better than the stuff they had back in town.

They started across the flat black cavern.

"If we're going to find another way out," Watch said, "we're going to have to explore every corner."

"How long will our light last?" Cindy asked.

"It's dimmed slightly since we entered here, but that's to be expected. There's nothing like fresh batteries. But I'd say we have at least another three hours of light."

"And after that?" Cindy asked.

"After that we'd better be back up at the door, or at

least to the steps. We couldn't walk for ten minutes in here without getting hopelessly lost."

"Better to be lost than stumble into the beast."

"It's too loud to stumble into," Watch said.

The beast got a lot louder a few minutes later.

7

THEY DIDN'T KNOW WHAT ACTUALLY WOKE
it up. Maybe it was simply time for it to get up. Maybe
it smelled them, or finally heard them. It didn't matter
really. All they knew was that when they were about ten
minutes from the dark pool, the breathing of the beast
changed. The monster sounded as if it were coughing,
and the faint red light that surrounded it suddenly flared.
In the ghastly light they saw a massive figure slowly stirring. But they could see no details of its appearance.
Cindy gasped and grabbed Watch's arm.

"Turn off your light!" she whispered.

"I just turned it off," he said calmly.

"Do you think it saw us?"

"I don't know. I don't want to ask it."

"What's it doing?" she asked.

"It sounds like it's getting out of bed."

"What should we do?"

"Nothing," Watch said.

"But we have to do something!"

"No. If we run back the way we came, we'll make more noise."

"Then let's walk back," Cindy said.

"No. I want to see what it's up to first."

"But we're exposed out here in the middle of nowhere!"

"We're assuming it's dangerous. It might be friendly. Let's be patient, and listen closely."

There were no more flares of light. They had to depend on their ears to monitor the creature's movements. From what they could tell, it seemed to be moving away from them, moving in the direction of the treasure room.

"If it is going in there," Cindy warned, "it'll freak out when it sees that two of its crystals have been stolen."

Watch slowly began to back up. "I agree. Maybe we should get out of here."

The roar came a minute later, and there was no mistaking its meaning. The beast had reached its private treasure chamber and found that a thief had slipped in while it slept. The sound of its anger reverberated throughout the black chamber like a volcanic eruption under a deep ocean. Worse, they heard it moving rapidly in their direction.

"It must know that the thief came in through the tunnel," Watch said.

"Who cares?" Cindy screamed. "Let's just get out of here!"

So they ran, back toward the steps and the long tunnel that led up to the closed door. But the beast was obviously fifty times their size and could move much more quickly than they could. And now there was no question as to whether it could hear them. It was obviously coming straight toward them, and the sound of its movements was terrifying. The very air seemed gripped by a deadly whirlwind. Watch and Cindy had to hold on to each other to keep from stumbling.

They were still a ways from the stairs when Watch realized they were not going to make it. The creature was seconds from reaching them, from crushing them as it clearly intended to do. But the dark pool was only a few feet up ahead and Watch pointed to it as they ran.

"We have to jump in there!" he yelled over the roar.

"What?"

"In there! We have to jump!"

"No! We'll die!"

"We're going to die before we reach the steps!" Watch tightened his hold on Cindy's hand. "We're jumping!"

"No!" Cindy screamed.

But they were already in the air, flying toward the water.

And it was a good thing.

Because from behind them a red wall of flame flashed forward. It was like the arm of an atomic bomb, and just as deadly. The fireball flew toward them with blinding speed. Just the heat of its approach was scalding. Watch and Cindy actually felt their skin begin to singe the instant before they hit the water. Then they were sinking into the cold blackness.

Yet that didn't last.

The red flame blasted over the surface of the pool, turning it into a nightmarish pot of human stew. Through the glare of the fire they could see each other floating beneath the bubbling surface as they heard the explosion of steam when the top few inches above the pool ruptured into gas. The steam, shot through with the fire, looked like a cloud from hell. The buoyancy of their bodies began to pull them to the surface but Watch reached over and yanked

Cindy back down. In the blistering red light, he frantically shook his head no.

His meaning was clear.

If we surface we get cooked.

The wall of flame began to dissipate but then another came and once more the surface exploded with steam. This time the blast from the superheated water began to reach them, and they had to swim deeper to keep from being scalded. But now they were each desperate for a breath. Watch pointed to the side and shook his arm. Once more his meaning was clear. They had to swim away from the boiling water before they could surface. Cindy shook her head frantically.

She wanted to go up.

Even though it meant she would be burned.

She just wanted to breathe.

But Watch wouldn't let her go up. He knew if they could just get a little ways from the fireball, the water would be a safe temperature. He shook his head firmly and continued to pull on Cindy's arm. But this struggle cost them both energy—and oxygen—and even Watch began to despair of getting to cooler water. His chest was a furnace in itself. He needed to breathe!

A third fire ball did not come.

The red light overhead began to diminish.

Suddenly they encountered cool water.

Cindy jerked to go up.

Watch jerked her back down. He flashed five fingers at her.

Let's move over five more feet.

He knew it could mean the difference between having the skin melted from their limbs and coming up in nice cool water. But he practically had to drag Cindy with him. But then, finally, they did surface, in warm water. As they gasped for air—and it had never felt so good to breathe—he put his hand half over her mouth.

"Breathe quietly," he whispered. "She's still close."

Cindy nodded as she tread water. Nearby the clouds of steam continued to glow a gruesome red, but the light was fading fast. If they could elude the beast a few more seconds, they might fool it into thinking they had perished.

But for all they knew the creature could see in the dark.

"Do you know where she is?" Cindy whispered when she had caught her breath.

Watch gestured back the way they had come. "Over there. She seems to be moving away."

"She's growling."

"She's mad," Watch said. "Her home has been broken into and her things disturbed."

Cindy pointed to the steps that ran through the center of the pool.

"Maybe we should make a run for the tunnel," she suggested.

"We'll take your earlier suggestion. We'll try walking there quietly."

While the beast lumbered about in the vast cavern, growling to itself, they climbed onto the path. They were drenched but far from cold because the water was now hotter than most Jacuzzis. In all the excitement, Watch had managed to hold on to the flashlight. But he couldn't turn it on to see if it was still working.

"We just have to follow the stone path," he said. "We can do without light for a few minutes."

Cindy clutched his arm. "Thank you for saving our lives. I would never have thought of jumping in the pool."

"I haven't saved anyone yet," Watch said.

They moved toward the tunnel at what they thought was a cautious and quiet pace. Yet once more they realized the beast had become aware of them and had begun to rush their way. But it had taken too long for her to realize they were still alive, so they were able to run far into the tunnel before the monster could unleash another fireball. In fact, she didn't even bother to try to kill them this time, when she saw how far into the tunnel they had climbed. She just smashed her massive face against the tunnel opening and then turned away in disgust.

It was then that Watch did something quite remarkable. Insane, Cindy thought at the time. Watch stopped running up the steps and turned to speak to the monster.

"Hello!" he called back down the steps. "We didn't take your crystals."

The beast stopped. A huge shadow of a face appeared at the end of the tunnel. Once more, they could see only a few details: a large scaly snout, dripping gold teeth, sharp purple ears. It was only the faint red light cast by her smoldering nostrils that allowed them to see anything. Yet the creature's eyes seemed to shine with their own light. They were as green and clear as the fairest emerald, and as massive as the largest TV screen. Overall the creature was larger than the biggest dinosaurs they had fought.

"Do you know what it is?" Watch whispered to Cindy.

"No. I don't have my encyclopedia of monsters with me. Why did you talk to it?"

"It's a dragon."

"No. There are no dragons."

"I am beginning to believe there is just about

everything. This is definitely a dragon. And I called out to her because I wanted her to know we didn't steal her crystals. I want to talk to her."

"Dragons can talk?" Cindy asked.

"They're supposed to be able to. They're supposed to be very smart. But you have to be careful when you speak to them, the old books say. They can hypnotize you."

"I'll let you do all the talking," Cindy said.

"Fine." Watch raised his head. Once more he shouted down to the dragon. "Do you understand English?"

There was a long pause, so long it seemed the creature could not possibly have understood him. But then she replied and her voice was as wonderful and as terrifying as her physical form. Her tone was as deep as a well and as powerful as thunder. Yet there was a gentleness to it, too, a subtlety that perhaps could hypnotize. Watch and Cindy listened as if struck.

"Yes, I understand your tongue," she said. "Long before you were born I lived across the sea, where they also spoke English. That was in a green land filled with green hills and many lovely trees. But your accent is yet strange to me. What do you call yourselves?"

"My name is Watch and this is my friend, Cindy. What's your name?"

"I was called Harome by the Englishmen, a name that sounded like both my large size and fiery temper. But I never liked that name, and I prefer you call me Slatron, which is the name I was given at birth, many of your centuries ago."

"Hi, Slatron," Cindy said, despite her vow to remain silent.

Watch spoke carefully. "We just wanted you to know that we're sorry that we woke you up, and that we didn't steal your crystals."

"Do you know who did steal them?" the dragon asked in a soft voice.

"Leah," Cindy blurted out.

"Shh," Watch whispered. "Be careful."

But Slatron was interested. "Who is this Leah?"

"Well," Watch said, also finding the dragon's mysterious voice hard to resist, but at least he was aware of the fact. "She's this girl we know. She's the one who led us here."

"Where is she now?" Slatron asked casually.

"She's heading back to town," Cindy said.

"I told you not to speak," Watch hissed at her.

Cindy fidgeted. "I don't want to lie to it."

"You don't need to lie to me," Slatron said in her soothing voice. "Just tell me what I need to know, and then there will be no danger for you. Where is this town you speak of?"

"It's not far from here," Watch said vaguely.

"What is it called?"

"Spooksville," Watch said. "At least that's what all of us kids call it. Its real name is Springville. But like I was saying, the town is not important. Getting your crystals back is all that matters, and we can help you do that."

"How can you help me?"

"If you would just open the door at the end of the tunnel," Watch said, "we could go out and find our friends."

"Your friends?" Slatron asked. "You have more than one friend? More than this Leah?"

"Leah is not our friend," Cindy blurted out.

"Yet she led you here you say," Slatron replied slowly. "Led you here to this place of great wealth. Are you sure you and your friends are not working with this Leah?"

"We are sure," Watch said with great difficulty. It was as if the dragon's voice were speaking from deep inside his brain, and he couldn't disagree with what she said, or withhold information from her. Yet he knew it could be dangerous to point the dragon toward Spooksville, or toward his other friends. Clearly the dragon could cause massive destruction with little effort.

"If you want to leave here," Slatron said, "I can show you

another way out. All you have to do is walk down here."

"Okay," Cindy said, taking a step forward. Watch grabbed her arm.

"What are you doing?" he whispered.

"I want to get out of here," she said. "The dragon knows another way out."

"But if you go down there the dragon might kill you."

Cindy seemed puzzled. "It seems friendly enough."

"You can trust me," Slatron said, obviously overhearing them. "My word is as good as gold. Come down here so I can show you the way out. Then we can talk about Leah and your other friends."

Watch continued to hold on to Cindy. "No," he said.

Slatron paused. "Why do you say no?"

Watch swallowed. He had to strain to do what he wanted and not what the dragon wanted.

"We don't want to come down there because we fear you might harm us," Watch explained. "But that doesn't mean we don't want to help you."

"We can only help each other if we trust each other," Slatron said. "Come down here now and I will help you in every way I can."

"No," Watch repeated.

"Watch," Cindy said, trying to pull away. "We should do what she says."

He had to pull her back up a step. "No. We can talk to her from up here. We're safe up here."

"But how long can you remain there?" Slatron asked. "Soon you will need food and water. I have both down here, plenty for both of you. Come to me and you can relax and eat and we can talk of the crystals your friends took from me."

"We told you," Watch said. "Leah took the crystals. She's not our friend."

"But you haven't told me exactly where this Leah is," the dragon replied, sharpening her tone. "I need to know. I need to speak to her."

"We don't know exactly where she is," Watch said. "But we have offered to look for her for you. If you'll just let us go."

"But if I let you go," Slatron said, "how do I know you will return with my treasure?"

"We promise," Cindy said.

"What if I go with you?" Slatron asked. "I haven't left here in a long time—a very long time. I would like to visit this Spooksville of yours. I would like to meet the people there."

"I don't think they'd want to meet you," Watch muttered.

"I heard that," Slatron said, sounding slightly

annoyed. "Now you begin to insult me, besides lie to me. I have offered to help you, and you have refused my help. I think perhaps you should remain here until I return with my crystals." The dragon paused and somehow wiggled one of her huge green eyes farther up the tunnel. It was literally impossible not to stare at it, to sink deep into its liquid green. Both Watch and Cindy felt pulled by its mysterious gaze into a void where they lost their own wills. Slatron added in a gentle voice, "I only need from you the direction your friends have gone."

Watch drew in a deep breath. "We can't tell you that."

"Why can't you tell me?" the dragon demanded quietly. "You must tell me. *Now.*"

"They went toward the o . . ." Cindy began, before Watch could clamp his hand over her mouth.

"We don't know where they went," Watch said quickly.

But the dragon was already chuckling. "They went toward the ocean? Is that the direction of this Spooksville? It would seem so, would it not, Cindy? Very good, I will go that way. But if you think you can escape while I am gone, think again. It will take you a long and hard search to find the other exit, and I will be back long before then, with your thieving friends. I must tell you it has been a long time since I enjoyed human meat, but enjoy it today I will!"

Watch started to protest, but the dragon had already made up her mind. To emphasize the fact, Slatron blasted a stream of fire in their direction. Like a river of rushing lava, the red mass flew up the stone steps and rebounded off the hard walls. Even though the flames did not touch them, the heat from the blast forced them back and let them know that they were prisoners of an old and deadly foe.

"That creature could devastate an entire town in a few minutes," Watch whispered as the flames died down. Cindy cringed by his side.

"But I told it Leah was the thief," she said.

"I don't think Slatron cares." Watch sighed. "We told the dragon too much."

8

ADAM, SALLY, AND BRYCE WERE LESS THAN
halfway to the truck—or where they hoped the truck
was still parked—when Slatron attacked them. One
minute they were hurrying along worried about their
friends trapped back in the cave, and the next they had
a fire-breathing lizard descending on them from above.
Sally saw the dragon first and pointed at her in horror.

"What the heck is that?" she screamed.

"Looks like a dragon," Bryce said.

"Looks like the ancient female pet we woke up,"
Adam said.

Sally grabbed Adam's arm. "It looks like she's mad!
Let's get out of here!"

They were lucky there was a series of caves nearby. They had their pick so naturally they chose the nearest one. They were barely into the shelter when a massive ribbon of flame poured across the cave opening. No fire touched them but the heat from the blast was painful. Particularly when the dragon made pass after pass through the air. The cave was not deep, so even when they huddled in the rear of it the superheated air was unbearable.

"Why doesn't she ask us what she wants?" Sally complained as the sweat ran down her face. The guys were in as bad shape. They knew they couldn't stay in the cave forever.

"She wants her crystals back," Adam said. "Isn't that obvious?"

"Perhaps we can reason with her," Bryce said. "Dragons are supposed to be very intelligent."

"Says who?" Sally said. "Who do you know who's ever talked to a dragon?"

"I've read books on the subject," Bryce said impatiently.

"Talk to her then," Adam said. "Just don't get yourself killed."

Bryce glanced at the burning cave entrance. "I can't just walk out there and talk to her."

"Coward," Sally said.

"He's not a coward," Adam said in Bryce's defense. "I meant he should try to talk to her from inside here. Look, I'll try. I'll call out to her. Dragons are supposed to have good hearing."

"And where did you learn that?" Sally demanded.

"I think Watch told me," Adam said.

"He was the one who gave me books on dragons," Bryce said.

"Hello!" Adam shouted through the flames that covered the cave entrance. "We don't have your crystals!"

The dragon ceased swooping by.

They thought they heard her land.

A moment later the most incredible face they had ever seen peered in through the cave entrance. Besides her incredible green eyes, she had magnificent scales, which seemed to sparkle like polished metal. The color of her hide changed in the shifting sunlight. Fortunately she was much too large to enter the cave. Yet she fastened them with her green eyes before speaking, and they felt as if a large portion of the dragon's will had walked right up to them and knocked them on the head. Adam had to force himself not to look directly at the beast.

"My name is Slatron," the dragon said in a

bewitching voice. "I have already spoken to your friends, Watch and Cindy. They say your friend Leah has stolen my crystals."

"That was nice of them," Bryce muttered sarcastically.

"That's true," Sally piped up. "She's the thief. How are Watch and Cindy doing by the way, Mrs. Slatron?"

"It is *Ms.* Slatron," the dragon replied. "Your friends are my prisoners, and if you don't tell me what I want to know, I will have them for dinner."

"You mean you will have them over for dinner?" Sally asked hopefully.

"I will eat them alive!" the dragon replied, sharpening her tongue. "You tell me now where this Leah is or you, too, will die!"

"Don't answer," Bryce said quickly. "She will just kill Leah when she finds her."

"But she will kill us if we don't answer," Sally said.

"She's bluffing," Bryce said. "She can't reach us in here."

"But she can make it hotter than it is in here," Adam said. "We can't take a much higher temperature. I think she knows that."

"We can't just turn Leah over to her," Bryce said.

"Sure we can," Sally said.

"Let me try to reason with the dragon," Adam said, turning back to the cave entrance. Immediately he felt the power of the dragon's eyes again. But he found if he forced himself to keep blinking, he didn't become hypnotized. He spoke in a reasonable tone.

"To be frank, Slatron, we do not know exactly where Leah is. We were looking for her when you showed up. And we will continue looking for her if you let us go. We are as anxious to find the crystals as you are. We have every intention of returning them to you. But we can't help you if you kill us, or hurt our friends. So why don't we try to work together on this, okay?"

The dragon continued to stare at them.

"I would like to work with you," Slatron said in a calm voice. "Why don't you step out here right now and we can talk about this partnership? You can lead me to Leah and I will have my crystals back and then I will be able to reward you with gems from my hidden treasure. All will be well. Come out here right now and we can talk."

"Don't listen to her!" Bryce hissed. "She has a snake's tongue. She is trying to confuse us. She will kill us if we go out there."

"You can understand that we are reluctant to come out right at this moment," Adam said to the dragon. "But we do want to help you. Even though we're just kids, we're very resourceful. We have saved whole civilizations from ruin. Hey, I have an idea. Why don't you return to your underground chamber for the time being and we'll return there in the next few hours with a progress report? We're sure to find Leah soon enough."

"No!" the dragon roared. "You will take me to her now!"

"We told you," Bryce said impatiently. "We don't know where she is."

"I know where she is!" the dragon yelled. "She has gone to Spooksville! I now know of this famous town. It lies by the ocean, and it is there I will go now! And it is there many will die until my crystals are returned!"

To show that she was not kidding, the dragon showered them with fire. Even though the flames did not reach the gang, the increase in temperature was intolerable to them. Adam felt as if he had been thrown onto a frying pan. Sweat no longer dripped from his face. He was past that stage. It was as if all the liquid had evaporated from his system, and he felt himself passing out.

It was Sally who saved them.

Sally still had her backpack. Adam and Bryce had left theirs behind to lighten their load so they could move faster. But Sally had been unwilling to part with her equipment—it cost too much, she had said—and now they realized it was a good thing. Her tent was coated with a thin layer of aluminum-like substance that was perfect for deflecting the summer heat—and bad dragon breath. As the boys swooned under the unceasing blast from Slatron's flames, Sally had the wits to rip open her pack and throw the tent over the three of them.

Immediately the temperature seemed to fall. Yet it took almost a minute before the dragon ceased her attack. She howled at them bitterly because she realized she was not going to be able to kill them as she had intended. The flames ceased and they were able to peek over the edge of the protective tent.

"I will come back for you when I have cooked Leah!" Slatron promised. "When I have destroyed all that you know, I will return for you and make you pay for what you have done to me and my family!"

"Wait!" Adam cried as the dragon turned to fly away.

Sally poked him in the side.

"Let the stupid dragon go," she said. "I am hot enough as it is."

"But we need to talk to her," Adam complained, uselessly. The dragon had already turned and flown off into the air.

"I hope Leah has already reached the truck," Bryce muttered.

"I don't know if her truck can outrun a dragon," Sally said.

"You would like that, wouldn't you?" Bryce said bitterly. "To see her killed for making a simple mistake."

Sally spoke patiently. "No, I do not want the dragon to kill Leah. Half of what I say I say because I get annoyed. My annoyance is the result of my biochemistry and I'm not personally responsible for it. Anyway, I hope she's reached the truck by now. I'd never wish an early death on anyone, particularly a good-looking teenager. But the truth of the matter is I am more concerned about what this dragon will do to Spooksville. Thousands might die because of what Leah has done."

"That's the reason we have to stop this dragon," Adam said. "Let's assume Leah does get to the truck. How can we stop her from leaving this area with the crystals?"

"I don't know how to stop her," Bryce said. "But at least I know how to contact her. Leah has her own cell phone and took it with her in the truck. I have another cell phone in some supplies I buried not far from here."

"Why do you have supplies buried way the heck up here?" Sally wanted to know.

"Because I am constantly battling forces of evil and need supplies at a moment's notice," Bryce explained.

"Oh," Sally said. "That makes good sense."

"How far are your supplies from here?" Adam asked.

"A half mile," Bryce said. "They're buried close to a narrow river that runs out of the mountains. I have a raft buried as well. If we can inflate it and ride the river out of here, we might be able to get back to Spooksville before the dragon. Let's hope Cindy and Watch wouldn't have told her precisely where it is located. Even though the dragon can fly, she will still have to search for the city."

"Why do you have a raft buried with your supplies?" Sally wanted to know.

"Because I can't swim," Bryce said.

Sally laughed. "You can save the world but you can't swim? I love it. Really, that's amazing. You are a superhero, no question about it."

"Enough," Adam said. "Let's get out of here."

The half mile passed quickly because they ran it. Not only did Bryce have a cell phone and a raft, he had a pump as well. While Adam and Sally worked to inflate the raft, Bryce tried calling his cousin. She answered right away. Apparently she was in the truck and driving back to town without them. Bryce spoke to her in an urgent tone.

"Leah," he said, "we know you stole the crystals. You have to bring them back."

There was a long pause. "I didn't take anything."

"We took the same route you did," Bryce said. "We entered the treasure chamber. We saw the empty grooves on top of the silver pedestal. You can't lie to us. You have to bring them back."

"Why should I?" she asked in an annoyed voice.

"Because the creature that was sleeping down there has awakened," Bryce said. "It's a dragon and she's looking for you. She's in the sky not far from where we are, but she moves fast and knows your name."

There was another pause. "I don't believe it. There are no dragons."

"You know I wouldn't lie to you," Bryce said. "But I am hurt that you lied to all of us. Why did you do it? Why did you run off without us?"

Leah spoke with emotion, with deep pain.

"Because the treasure is mine. Father gave it to me. And it's all that I have left in the world now that he's dead."

Bryce replied gently. "Then why did you show us the map at all? It's obvious to us now that you understood the clues all along."

"I didn't know how to reach the Teeth."

"You could have figured it out, asked around. Tell me the real reason, Leah?"

She considered. On the other end of the line, she

could have been biting her lip. "I was afraid," she said finally. "I thought I needed your help. But when I saw the peak standing there so close, last night, I thought I could do it by myself. And I did, Bryce. I brought out half of the greatest treasure the place had to offer."

"But you don't even know what you've got," Bryce said into the phone. "None of us does."

"The map said the crystals are magical, and I believe it. I just have to figure out how to use them."

"You have to figure out how to survive," Bryce said. "Look out your window, Leah. The dragon is coming for you."

There was another long pause.

"I don't see anything, cousin," Leah replied. "Anyway, I'll hit Coast Highway soon enough. Then nothing can catch me." She paused. "I'm sorry, Bryce. You're a good kid. I didn't want to hurt you."

"You're hurting more than me," Bryce pleaded. "The dragon swore she would torch the town. Thousands could die."

Leah seemed to sniff.

"Since dad died," she said, "I have realized one thing. I have to look out for myself first. No one else is going to."

"Leah," Bryce said.

His cousin had already hung up.

Sally looked at Bryce with sympathy.

"No luck?" she asked.

Bryce set the phone down. "Let's get this raft in the water."

9

WHEN SLATRON LEFT, WATCH TOLD CINDY
they had to search the underground chamber once more.
But Cindy was afraid to leave the safety of the tunnel.

"The dragon could return at any second," she said.
"At least she can't get to us here."

"But here is nowhere," Watch said. "The creature was
right—eventually we'll need food and water. But if we
find the exit while she's gone, we stand a chance."

"But the dragon said it was next to impossible to find
the way out."

"Dragons lie. She wants you to feel hopeless. But if
there's an exit down here big enough to let that creature
out, then we'll find it. Let's get to it."

Cindy grabbed his arm. "Are we sure she's gone?"

Watch shared the same concern. "We can't be sure of anything at this point."

They walked back down the steps, for the third time. Once clear of the tunnel, they stood still and waited for the dragon to strike. But it seemed as if indeed they were alone. Now they had to make a crucial decision. Which way to head?

"I think we should go the other way," Cindy suggested. "Away from the treasure chamber. Away from where the dragon slept."

"Good idea," Watch said. "We need to explore fresh territory."

At first the way was the same as the other—flat and barren and dark. But then they came to what appeared to be a wide winding road. It spiraled upward and for that reason they believed that they were closing in on the exit. But the climbing was difficult. They had not rested properly the night before, and the day had been stressful. They breathed hard as they climbed.

"How are your legs?" Watch asked.

"Tired. Sore."

"I think we're going to make it."

"Do you really?" she asked. "Or are you saying that to keep me from breaking down?"

"A little of both." He added, "I've never seen you break down under pressure."

She laughed softly. "This town does give you a thick skin. Do you think other kids in any other part of the country go through half of what we do in a typical week?"

"I couldn't imagine it if they do," Watch said.

An hour later they paused to take a break. They were halfway through their water bottles, which they had once more filled at the dark pool. But climbing was thirsty work. It was while they were resting that they heard a strange sound in front of them.

"What was that?" Cindy asked, jumping.

Watch turned off the flashlight. "It was something."

"Could the dragon be back already?" she asked anxiously.

"It's possible."

"We should run back to the tunnel!"

"Shh. We're both exhausted. We wouldn't be able to run that far. Besides, the sound could be something other than the dragon." Watch stood in the pitch-black and then finally stepped forward. "Let me check it out."

Cindy grabbed him, having to find him by touch alone.

"No," she said. "We're not separating."

"All right." He patted her on the back. "I know you're scared, Cindy. I'm scared, too. But I think we have to risk it and go forward. To return to the cave is all but a death sentence. We'll get trapped there, and then we'll be at the mercy of the dragon."

Cindy nodded. "Then if we're going forward, turn the light back on. Darkness won't save us. The dragon will hear us coming. At least this way we can see what we're up against."

"Agreed." Watch flipped on the flashlight.

Their next steps were the hardest ones of their lives.

They heard their breathing, their hearts pounding.

And something else. Yes, something big—definitely big.

Stirring in the dark in front of them.

Finally the beam from their flashlight fell on it.

All hope died inside them.

They knew they were dead.

It was another dragon.

"Oh no," Cindy moaned.

Watch hugged her to his side. "Close your eyes."

But neither of them closed them.

The dragon spoke. He spoke modern-day English.

He sounded more like a kid than an ancient monster.

"Hi," he said happily. "Who are you?"

Watch almost choked on his own voice he was so

relieved to hear the welcoming tone. "I am Watch," he said. "This is my friend, Cindy. Who are you?"

"Harve," the dragon said and offered a sharp-clawed talon. "Pleased to meet you."

They stared at his huge claw. "Would it be okay if we didn't shake just now?" Watch asked. "We don't mean to be rude."

Harve withdrew his claw. "Sorry. I guess my hand is too big for you guys. Hey, how did you get in here? Did you take the tunnel down here?"

"Yes," Cindy muttered.

"Cool," Harve said. "I have been hoping somebody would use that tunnel one day."

"How long have you been down here?" Watch asked.

The dragon seemed to shrug. He was not nearly so big as Slatron.

"I don't know," he said. "Maybe five hundred years."

"But you sound so young," Cindy said.

Harve nodded. "Dragons grow slowly. I didn't learn to walk until I was a hundred. My mom thought I would never learn to talk."

"But you speak good English," Watch said.

"Thank you. My mom says it's the language most people use nowadays so she taught it to me."

"Is your mother Slatron?" Cindy asked.

"That's her. We're the only dragons who live here. I guess you must have met her?"

"We sure did," Watch said. "She tried to kill us."

Harve seemed to frown. "Oh. Sorry about that. You must have made her mad. What did you do, play with her treasure?"

"This girl we know stole a few pieces of her treasure," Cindy explained. "Two of her crystals."

Harve snorted. "That explains it. She loves those crystals almost as much as she loves me."

"What are they?" Watch asked. "What can they do?"

"You can talk to anyone anywhere anytime if you have them," Harve explained. "As long as the other person has one as well. My mom uses them to talk to dragons on other planets."

"She talks to other planets!" Cindy said, astounded.

"She has to," Harve said. "There aren't many dragons to talk to here."

"I see your point," Watch said.

"Hey," Harve said. "Do you know where my mom went? I haven't been able to find her."

"She left this mountain in order to torch our friends and our city," Cindy said. "We need to stop her. Can you help us?"

"I can try," Harve said pleasantly. "I like humans more

than my mom does. I want to tell you right now that I've never eaten a person. I'm a vegetarian."

"That's good to know," Watch said. "Can we communicate with your mother right now using one of the crystals?"

"Not unless she's got one with her," Harve said.

Cindy looked at Watch. "Slatron left here in a hurry," she said. "I doubt she took a crystal with her."

"I'm sure she didn't," Watch said. "But Leah has two with her. We might be able to talk her into bringing them back."

"That sounds like the best plan," Harve said. "Once my mom gets in a bad mood, it's hard to calm her down. The only thing that will cool her off is to see the crystals again."

"Let's go to the treasure chamber," Watch said. "We'll see if Leah will answer us."

"Are you guys tired?" Harve asked. "Would you like a ride there?"

"You don't mind?" Cindy asked. "We are exhausted."

"Not at all," Harve said. "I love giving humans rides."

They climbed up on the dragon's back.

"Have you seen many humans before?" Watch asked.

"A few. Nice creatures."

"Where are they now?" Cindy asked.

Harve lowered his voice as he lowered his wings for them.

"I'm not sure," he said with a note of reluctance. "I think my mom ate them."

In the treasure chamber Harve explained how to use the crystals to communicate with Leah.

"Hold one in your right hand and think of her," he said. "Then begin to speak. If she has a crystal nearby, she will hear you."

Watch picked up a crystal and offered it to Cindy.

"Do you want to try to reason with her?" he asked.

Cindy shook her head. "No."

"I'll try it then." Watch held the crystal tight and closed his eyes. He had no trouble visualizing Leah. Indeed, the image of her face and other features popped into his mind with unusual clarity. He wondered if the crystal was responsible. It seemed to boost the power of his thoughts. He spoke in a soft but clear voice. "Leah," he said. "Can you hear me?"

There was a long pause. Then a worried voice seemed to speak from the center of the room. "Who's there?" Leah asked.

"It's me, Watch. I am speaking to you via the crystals. They are interstellar communication devices, but they can also be used to make local calls."

There was another pause.

"I don't believe it," Leah said.

"It's true," Watch said. "How else could you hear me? But I don't want to argue about that right now. We need you to bring those crystals back. You see, there's this dragon looking for them and she's in a really bad mood. If she finds you, she'll probably kill you."

"Are you calling for Bryce?" Leah asked impatiently. "He just called an hour ago and said the same thing. I hung up on him."

"He was telling you the truth. Where are you right now?"

"Why should I tell you?" Leah said. "I'm home free, that's where I am. If these crystals are so magical then I should be able to sell them for millions of dollars. I won't have to worry about working the rest of my life. That's why my father gave me the treasure map, you know. He wanted me to be taken care of. I don't know why all of you are treating me like a criminal."

"We don't judge you for wanting financial security," Watch said. "We're just worried about this angry dragon. When she left here, she said she was going to wipe out our friends and all of Spooksville."

"Your friends are with Bryce and they are fine," Leah said. "But Spooksville is going to have to take care of itself. I am not going to return my inheritance."

"But you didn't inherit these crystals," Watch said.

The connection was abruptly broken.

The strong image of Leah vanished from Watch's mind. He opened his eyes and spoke to Cindy and Harve. "I think she hung up on me," he said.

"I hate when that happens," Harve said sympathetically.

"What are we going to do?" Cindy asked. "We have to stop Slatron before she reaches Spooksville."

Watch spoke to Harve. "Can these crystals also be used as a homing device? Can we use them to locate Leah?"

"Yes," Harve said. "If these crystals move toward the other crystals, they will get warmer."

"But even if we know where she is," Cindy said, "how are we going to catch up to her?"

Watch studied Harve. "You say it took you a hundred years to learn to walk?"

The young dragon was embarrassed. "A hundred and twenty years to be exact."

"Can you fly?" Watch asked.

Harve stuttered. "I don't understand."

"You have wings. Do you know how to use them?" Watch asked.

"Yes. I can flap them." Harve flapped them to show he was not boasting. "I have very strong wings."

"But you haven't answered my question," Watch insisted. "Can you fly?"

Harve cleared his throat. "Yes. Of course. Sort of."

"You can either fly or you can't," Cindy said. "What's the matter?"

"Nothing."

"You seem uncomfortable talking about flying," Watch said.

"Well," Harve said quietly, lowering his head, "I can fly but I prefer not to. You know what I mean."

"We don't," Watch said. "Explain what you mean?"

"I'm afraid of heights," Harve mumbled.

"But you're a dragon," Cindy said. "How can you be afraid of heights?"

Harve was clearly humiliated. "That's what Mom always asks. But, I don't know, I just get scared when I get up high. I feel like I might fall and hurt myself."

Watch grabbed the other crystal from the silver pedestal. "Well, you're going to have to fly us to Leah now. Too many lives are at stake."

Harve buried his head under a wing. "I have to?" he asked in a worried voice.

Cindy stepped over and patted him on the shoulder. "Don't worry," she said. "We will be with you."

"Not that we'll be any help if you start to fall," Watch said.

10

AS THEY WERE FLOATING IN THEIR RAFT toward Spooksville, Sally came up with an idea to stop Slatron. "What are dragons supposed to love the most?" she asked Adam and Bryce.

"Treasure," Bryce said.

"Gold," Adam said.

"Exactly," Sally said. "Now this raft is going to float right by Spooksville's main electrical power plant. The power lines that run out of there pass over a stone ledge that isn't far from the plant gates. What if we get some paint and spray that ledge a bright gold? Maybe she'll see the gold, think it's treasure, and swoop down to peck at it. While she's doing that, we can hide in the rocks above the ledge and shoot out the power lines so they fall on her back. The high-powered electrical charge would kill a human, but will only knock her out so she can calm down. Bryce, I assume you can get hold of some gold paint and a laser-guided sniper's rifle?"

"I'll need a bit of time but I can get both," Bryce said, interested. "I like the plan."

Adam nodded reluctantly. "It could work. But I hate to hurt the dragon. We were the ones, after all, that invaded her home."

"And now she wants to destroy our home," Sally said seriously. "There is a time for quiet diplomacy and there is a time for full-throttle battle, Adam. We have no choice. We have to stop the dragon and we have to stop her now."

Adam nodded, "I suppose you're right. But I keep thinking how she mentioned her family."

"You saw her temper," Sally said. "If she has a husband then we are doing him a favor by knocking out his wife."

Adam sighed. "I don't think he would see it that way."

The current of the river was fast. They reached the power plant minutes later. Bryce disappeared, probably to dig up another one of his secret stashes. He wasn't gone long, and when he did return he had a rifle that looked as if it had been invented in a secret laboratory in the basement of the Pentagon. The bullets were as large as mustard jars. He also brought cans of gold paint and rollers.

"I couldn't find a spray gun on such short notice," he said as they rolled up their sleeves and began to paint the rocky ledge, just below the humming power lines.

"I guess you're not perfect, after all," Sally said.

"It's been a while since you thought I was perfect," Bryce grumbled.

Sally laughed and reached over and painted his right cheek gold.

"Cheer up," she said. "I'm only hard on you because I know you have potential."

They had their bait ready in less than thirty minutes. The painted ledge actually did look like—from a distance—a genuine vein of gold. Hiking away from the ledge, they huddled behind a bunch of nearby trees. Bryce carefully began to load his sniper rifle.

"Where did you get such a weapon?" Sally asked.

"That's classified information," Bryce muttered.

"I don't like guns," Adam said. "Certainly not in the hands of minors. There are laws against such things."

Bryce gave him a hard stare. "This town is about to

be attacked by a fire-breathing dragon and you are lecturing me on gun laws?"

Adam shrugged. "I just don't like guns. Too many accidents happen around them."

"Of course you do have a laser pistol in your chest of drawers in your bedroom," Sally said.

"That's different," Adam said defensively. "I only take it out when aliens invade the earth."

They had laid their trap none too soon. Slatron appeared a few minutes later. The sight of the gold definitely caught her eye, and she swooped down with red fire flaring from her nostrils. Bryce didn't give the dragon a second to examine the ledge. The moment the beast landed he sprung their trap. Using the laser-guided sight, he took aim at the power lines above the dragon and opened fire.

One of the power lines broke and fell on the dragon. Slatron howled in agony.

Bryce fired again and again, in quick succession.

Two more sparkling lines landed on the dragon and she rolled onto her side in pain. Apparently her thick scaly hide was no protection from the massive current that was now pouring through its body. Sally's brilliant plan was working, but even though she had thought it up, Adam saw her turn away with tears in her eyes. The dragon flopped on her back and kicked her legs as if she were suffering from a seizure. Even Bryce dropped his rifle.

"I wish there had been another way," he said. "But at least it's over."

Adam could not tear his eyes away from the horror. "Yeah," he said sadly. "It's over."

But Adam and Bryce were wrong.

A second dragon suddenly appeared in the sky. It swooped down toward Slatron and the crackling wires. It knocked the wires away from Slatron. Adam and his friends briefly wondered if they were in for another fire fight, but then they saw that the new dragon was carrying Watch and Cindy and Leah on its back. Sally blinked in amazement.

"This is too weird," she said. "Even for this town."

The new dragon landed nearby and Cindy, Watch, and Leah climbed off his back and ran toward their friends. Harve went to attend to Slatron, who was already recovering from the electrical shock. Slatron rolled onto her belly and Harve brushed her with his wings. Cindy and Watch were laughing as they walked up. Even Leah was smiling, although she seemed embarrassed to face Bryce.

"I can see you guys have been busy," Sally said.

Cindy gestured to the laser-assisted rifle and the downed electric wires.

"You don't look like you've been waiting around to be rescued," Cindy said.

Sally shrugged. "All in a day's work. But tell us how you got here."

"Harve brought us," Cindy said simply.

"Harve?" Bryce said.

"That kid dragon," Watch said, pointing. "He's pretty cool. He helped us catch up with Leah and then he bought the crystals back from her with his weekly allowance."

Sally frowned. "His allowance? What did he give you, Leah?"

Now they knew why Leah was smiling.

She held out a handful of beautiful diamonds.

"These," she said.

Adam had to laugh. "I wish I had an inheritance like that."

Leah shook her head. "This is no inheritance, and Harve didn't really buy the crystals from me. I gave them back when I heard how much they meant to his mother. I realized I was way off base taking them. I should never have taken them in the first place." Leah pointed to Slatron and her son. The electrical wires had been pushed farther away. Mother and child seemed to be doing well. They looked over and waved their wide wings, and Slatron didn't even appear to be mad anymore. Leah continued, "Harve simply gave me these gems as a favor when he heard I'd lost my father. He said he didn't want me poor and destitute."

Sally stared at the gems hungrily. "That Harve sounds like a nice guy. Would he like to do each of us a favor?"

But the gang didn't let Sally talk to the young dragon. They were too afraid of angering his mother again.

About the Author

CHRISTOPHER PIKE is the author of more than forty teen thrillers, including the Thirst, Remember Me, and Chain Letter series. Pike currently lives in Santa Barbara, where it is rumored he never leaves his house. But he can be found online at www.Facebook.com/ChristopherPikeBooks.